My Sister Says

Betty Baker

My Sister Says

Illustrated by Tricia Taggart

Macmillan Publishing Company
New York
Collier Macmillan Publishers
London

For
Verna Gulick
with love

Copyright © 1984 Betty Baker
Copyright © 1984 Tricia Taggart
All rights reserved. No part of this book may be reproduced
or transmitted in any form or by any means, electronic or
mechanical, including photocopying, recording or by any
information storage and retrieval system, without
permission in writing from the Publisher.
Macmillan Publishing Company
866 Third Avenue, New York, N.Y. 10022
Collier Macmillan Canada, Inc.
Printed in the United States of America
10   9   8   7   6   5   4   3   2   1
Library of Congress Cataloging in Publication Data
Baker, Betty.
My sister says.
Summary: In 1850's New York City, two sisters
fantasize about the gifts their sailor father might bring
home if he sailed to exotic places.
[1. New York (N.Y.)—Fiction. 2. Sisters—Fiction]
I. Taggart, Tricia, ill.   II. Title.
PZ7.B1693My   1984   [E]   83-911
ISBN 0-02-708160-5

Sometimes when Daddy is sailing home,
my sister says,
"Do you want to go and meet Daddy's ship?"
And I always say, "Yes!" just as loud as I can.

Then we take off our aprons and put on our bonnets.
And Momma tells us,
"Look out for horses and wagons and puddles."
Aunt Bell tells us, "Have a good time."
I have to look out for the wagons and puddles.
My sister is looking at all the fine ladies.

3

Then we come to the river
and both of us look at the tall ships.
"That ship," says my sister, "sails to China.
It brings back silk and tea and teapots."
There are dragons in China.
I saw a picture in a big blue dish.

My sister says, "If Daddy sailed to China,
he would bring me silk to make a dress."
He would bring me a dragon.

5

I would ride it up Broadway
and down Fifth Avenue.
People would say, "Give us a ride!"
And I would say, "Yes, for a penny."
Then I could get Daddy a present.

And if a policeman yelled and said,
"Get that dragon out of the street!"
I would go to the mayor and talk to him.
The mayor would say,
"What a fine idea, my dear!"
And he would hang a medal around my neck
so no policeman could yell at me.

Every day, when it got dark,
I would ride my dragon around New York.

My dragon would light all the street lights.
And every morning, when it got light,
I would ride around and blow them out.

My sister says,
"I would make a silk dress
  with a long, long train."
"It will get in the puddles," I tell her.
"But Daddy will bring me a dragon
  and you can ride on it for a penny."
"Don't be silly," my sister says.
"Daddy couldn't bring you a dragon.
  It would burn the sails and maybe the ship."
"He could bring me a baby dragon," I say.
"A baby dragon can't make much fire."
"It would grow up," my sister says.
"It takes a year and maybe more
  to sail to China and back."
I'm glad that Daddy does not sail to China
even if I never get a dragon.

"That ship," says my sister, "comes from India.
It brings carpets and cottons
and things made of ivory."
Some of the carpets in India can fly.
Aunt Bell told me a story about them.

My sister says, "If Daddy sailed to India,
he could bring me ivory.
Then I would make a fan to go with my dress."
He could bring me a flying carpet.

I would go into the big new hotel
and unroll my carpet at the foot of the stairs.
I would sit on it and tell the people,
"Ride up to your room for only a penny!"
And the people would say,
"What a wonderful way to go upstairs!
Every hotel should have something like this."
Maybe they would give me two pennies or three.
Then I could give Daddy a fine big present.

15

My sister says,

"With a silk dress and an ivory fan,

I could go to a ball at the new hotel."

"You can ride upstairs on my flying carpet.

It only costs a penny," I say.

"Don't be silly," my sister says.

"Carpets can't fly. That is only a story."

"Are you sure?" I say.

And my sister says, "If carpets could fly,

that ship would be on one.

It takes months and months to sail from India."

I am very sorry that carpets can't fly.

But I am glad that Daddy does not sail to India.

We see a ship with lots of people.
"That ship," says my sister, "is sailing out west,
way out west to California.
There is lots of gold in California."

There are lots of Indians way out west.
Everybody knows that.
If Daddy sailed there, he could bring me a tepee
and a long feather bonnet and a tom-tom
and war paint and a tomahawk.

I would set up the tepee in Washington Square.
I would paint my face and put on the bonnet.
And on sunny days, at half-past three,
I would do a war dance in front of the tepee.
People would clap and throw pennies at me.

My sister says, "I wish I had gold rings and a pin."

"You could play the tom-tom," I tell her.

"And I will give you half of the pennies."

"What pennies?" says my sister.

"The ones I will get for doing a war dance
after Daddy sails way out west," I say.

"Don't be silly," my sister says.

"A ship must sail around Cape Horn
to go to California.
It takes almost as long as sailing to India."

I am glad that Daddy does not sail out west.

But I would like to be an Indian some time.

Then we see a ship
that is not as tall or as wide as the others.
I say, "How far does that one sail?"

My sister says,
"Far up the river to towns and farms
to get apples and peaches, candy and wooden dolls."

I do not ask how long it takes.
I already know.
It takes days and days and sometimes weeks.
I am glad that Daddy does not have to sail
to China or India or way out west.

"There he is. Hurry!" says my sister.

"What's the matter?"

"I want to give Daddy a present," I say.

"But I don't have a dragon

or a flying carpet,

and I cannot dance without Indian things.

So I did not get pennies to buy him a present."

"Don't be silly," my sister says.

"The very best present is a hug and a kiss."

And it is.